AND THEN IT HAPPENED

9

M & L Wade

Books for Boys

ISBN 9780973117882

Printed in Canada by Hignell Book Printing

Books For Boys Inc.
P.O. Box 87
Strathroy ON N7G 3J1

Table of Contents

Chapter 1

The Sharks

On Monday morning, our principal announced that he had a surprise for everyone. He paused as the whole school waited to hear what it was.

"Hey," shouted Gordon. "I'll bet I know what the surprise is. Mr. Evans forgot to pay the rent, and the whole school is being evicted. Quick, everyone! Pack up your stuff and follow me. We're outta here!"

"Sit down and be quiet, Gordon," sighed our teacher, Mrs. Hoagsbrith.

Mr. Evans continued. "This past Saturday, the local

high school dodge ball team, the Rockets, took first place at the District Championship Tournament. The team is being flown to the Sea Land Resort to compete in the country's largest dodge ball tournament ever. There will be over 1000 teams competing. Many of the students on the local high school team are former Danglemore students, and this morning, right after announcements, they will be here in our gym to give us a demonstration of just how good they are!"

Every class in the school cheered, every class except ours. "But that's our gym period," we grumbled. "It's not fair. Why couldn't we miss something like math or geography instead?"

"Well," said Mrs. Hoagsbrith, sighing again. "Then that's today's first lesson. Life isn't fair."

Our class made its way to the gym. For 15 minutes we watched the high school team warm up while we waited for the rest of the school to file in and sit down. The team showed us how hard and fast they could throw the ball, and how they could skillfully dodge the balls that were being hurled at them. Gordon, Paulo and I agreed that they were very good.

When the whole school had finally assembled in the gym, the coach blew his whistle and the warm up was over. Our principal stood up and announced that the Rockets needed a team to play against to demonstrate their great skill, and since this was actually Mrs. Hoagsbrith's gym time, our class was chosen to play against the Rockets!   He beamed at us as if this were some great privilege. Our class stared at the ground. No one moved. None of us wanted to go up against the powerful high school team that we had just watched warm up. We would be creamed! Mrs. Hoagsbrith came to our defence.

"But my class is only half the size of these high school students, and they've had no special training or coaching!"

"Ahh, that doesn't matter," laughed Mr. Evans. "Trained or not, your class will be knocked out of the game in two minutes flat." The entire gym full of kids chuckled with laughter.

Our teacher was getting angry. "I didn't bring my kids down here to be used as target practice," she said. "And what if my kids *do* beat the high school team? Then what?"

"I don't think we need to worry about *that*," smirked Mr. Evans. "But, in the *unlikely* event that your kids win, I'll personally do all their homework for a month!"

At the thought of no homework for an entire month, our class jumped up and stampeded to the middle of the gym, ready to do battle with the high school champs.

Mrs. Hoagsbrith crossed her arms, shook her head and laughed in the principal's face. "You have no idea of the power you've just unleashed! No homework for a month... my kids will *slaughter* the high school team!"

Our class shouted war woops and victory chants at the Rockets, who looked surprised and even a little scared. Gordon raised his hand, and our class immediately became silent. Pointing to the Rockets' captain, he shouted, "Our team is called the Sharks, and you guys are going to lose big time!"

The referee blew his whistle and the game was on! The Rockets didn't stand a chance. Although they were far bigger and stronger than we were, as Mrs. Hoagsbrith later said, she never had a class where the kids worked so hard to do so little. Our class was determined to get out of doing homework for a full month, and *nothing* was going to stop us. While the Rockets took aim and threw the ball at us with amazing accuracy, we dove, dodged and rolled out of the way. Sometimes we caught the ball and whipped it back at them, knocking the Rockets over like bowling pins. Within minutes, we had cleared the floor of Rockets and won the game. The ref blew the whistle and declared the Sharks the winners! The gym went wild. The school cheered and stamped their feet, while Mrs. Hoagsbrith looked on with a satisfied grin on her face.

Patting Mr. Evans on the back, she said, "The Rockets never stood a chance. You see, my class will do *anything* to get out of homework. When it comes to avoiding work, my kids are Number 1!"

"Did you hear that?" yelled Gordon. "We're Number 1! We're Number 1!" The entire gym took up the chant.

When we finally got back to our classroom, another surprise awaited us. The organizers of the dodge ball tournament had been in the gym watching the game, and they said that because we had beaten the Rockets so easily, the high school team was being pulled out of the tournament, and we would be allowed to go in their place. The Sharks would be given an all-expenses paid trip to the Sea Land Resort instead of the Rockets!

*   *   *   *   *

The following Saturday, Mrs. Hoagsbrith, our entire class, and many parents were flown first class to the Sea Land Resort for the big dodge ball tournament. From the airport, we were taken by an air-conditioned bus to the resort.

When the bus came to a stop in front of a large, beautiful building, our teacher said to the bus driver, "I think we're at the wrong place. See the sign? It says 'Welcome to Sea Land'. We're not going to Sea Land. We're going to the Sea Land *Resort*."

"This *is* the Sea Land Resort," said the bus driver. "Look at the sign again. The word 'Resort' is just burned out."

We all looked, and it was true. We were at the Sea Land Resort; you just couldn't read the word 'Resort.'

"And look," said Gordon, pointing excitedly. "See the

smaller sign underneath? It says 'Welcome Sharks!' That's us!"

"Sea Land is just down the road," explained the bus driver. "That's where they keep all the marine animals. You should visit it while you're here if you have time."

We thanked the bus driver and climbed off of the bus. The Sea Land Resort was a beautiful hotel, but the best part of all was the huge indoor/outdoor swimming pool with water slides and the highest diving board I had ever seen. We couldn't wait to get to our rooms and change into our bathing suits! A sharp whistle from Mrs. Hoagsbrith stopped us in our tracks.

"The coach and I have already discussed things with your parents, and we agreed that you need to save your strength for the tournament tomorrow. Therefore, no one is allowed in the pool until after the tournament. You must all go to your rooms now and get some rest."

"Only adults could ruin a good time at a great place like this," grumbled Gordon as we reluctantly crowded into the elevators.

To make matters worse, the room that Gordon, Paulo

and I were sharing overlooked the pool. From our window we could see Mrs. Hoagsbrith, the coach and our parents below us, happily splashing and diving into the pool. Several mothers lounged on the deck, tall colourful drinks in their hands. When we saw our teacher laughing as she slid down one of the many slides, landing in the pool with a huge splash, Gordon said, "That's it! We've got to do something!"

"What can we do?" I asked. "The parents will just send us back to our rooms if we try to get into the pool."

"Only if they catch us," said Gordon. "We'll wait until they've all gone to bed. Then we'll all sneak down into the pool and have a good time."

"But what if they hear us?" said Paulo.

"We'll be real quiet," said Gordon. "Let's round up everyone and hold a meeting in our room. It's time our class had some fun! If it weren't for us, *they* wouldn't even be here."

Ten minutes later, our entire class had gathered in our hotel room for an emergency meeting.

"As you know," began Gordon, "the teacher, the coach

and our parents think that we kids should be resting before the tournament begins tomorrow. Well, we didn't rest before we beat the Rockets at school, and I don't think we need to rest up now. I think that was just an excuse to get us out of the way so they could have the pool all to themselves."

Several kids nodded in agreement and a few looked downright angry. How dare the adults force us into these air-conditioned rooms where there was nothing to do but watch TV and movies and play video games. As usual, we thought, adults took care of themselves first and kids last.

"Okay, so here's the plan," continued Gordon. "We'll wait until all of the adults have left the pool, and then we'll give them another half hour to make sure they're asleep. Then we'll quietly sneak down to the pool and have our turn."

It was agreed that Gordon, Paulo and I would keep an eye on the pool through our hotel room window, and a half hour after the parents had gone to bed, we would tiptoe down the hall and knock three times on everyone's door. That was the signal to meet at the pool. It was a great plan. As long as we were quiet, what could possibly go wrong?

About an hour later, the adults finally got tired and headed to their hotel rooms for the night. Gordon, Paulo and I waited another half hour before we began knocking quietly on the other kids' doors to let them know that it was our turn to use the pool.

*   *   *   *   *

Meanwhile, someone else was getting ready to use the pool as well. More specifically, *something* else was getting ready to use the pool, and that *something* was two great white sharks.

Earlier that day, far out in the ocean, some fishermen had accidentally caught two big sharks in their nets. Knowing that Sea Land was looking to add some great white sharks to their collection, the fishermen decided to donate the sharks instead of throwing them back into the ocean. They called Sea Land and were told, "Great! Bring them right over and dump them in the pool marked *Sharks*."

10

Now, just as our class was sneaking out of our hotel rooms to have some fun in the pool, a truck with the two sharks pulled up and stopped in front of our hotel. The truck driver read the sign that said 'Sea Land' and 'Welcome Sharks.'

"*This must be the place*," he thought, not noticing the burned out word 'Resort.' The man backed up his trailer and dumped the two huge sharks into the hotel swimming pool. They entered the pool with a loud splash and made their way to the bottom of the pool, *where they were now swimming around in circles looking for something to eat.* The truck driver drove off into the night, whistling to himself, happy to have given the sharks a new home.

Minutes later, our class came silently sneaking into the pool area, towels in hand and ready for some fun.

Since the plan had been Gordon's idea, the class decided to let him be the first to jump off the high diving board, and then the rest of us would follow him into the pool. As Gordon quickly climbed the tall ladder leading to the diving board, the sharks caught his movement and waited in the deep water below, toothy jaws wide open.

Gordon walked to the end of the diving board and jumped up and down a few times as he prepared to dive into the glistening water. Unseen below, the sharks circled in anticipation. With a final spring, Gordon leapt off the board and dove headfirst into the water. And then it happened.

Both sharks, eager to be the first to eat Gordon, swam up toward him with their mouths open. Spotting the sharks as he entered the water, Gordon immediately began kicking like crazy to get to the surface of the water and out of the pool. The sharks leapt out of the water and came down, jaws first, aiming straight for Gordon. Seeing the sharks coming at him, Gordon frantically dove sideways. The hungry sharks landed on top of him, and the three of them disappeared into the deep, bubbling water of the pool. Seconds later, the sharks leapt out of the water and every kid in our class stared in silent amazement as we saw the terrified Gordon on the back of the largest shark, riding him bucking-bronco style, holding on for dear life.

Every kid in the class started screaming and throwing

anything they could get their hands on at the sharks, trying to save Gordon. Deck chairs, tables, and umbrellas were hurled into the pool, missing the sharks but not Gordon, who was struck several times by flying objects.

Our screaming and shouting brought the parents and our teacher running into the pool area in their pajamas to break up what they no doubt thought was a huge, out-of-control party.

Without her glasses, Mrs. Hoagsbrith squinted and saw Gordon riding on the back of *something.* She immediately assumed that this was a game he was playing while the rest of us cheered him on.

"Gordon Smith, get off that pool toy and get out of the water this instant!" she bellowed.

At that moment, the shark leapt out of the water and gave a tremendous shake, causing Gordon to fly through the air and crash land on the deck of the pool, gasping for breath and shaking with fear.

Every kid in the class rushed over to Gordon to make sure he was unharmed. The parents stared at the scene with utter disbelief and confusion.

The next instant, several security people from the resort ran into the pool area, blowing whistles. They stopped in their tracks when they spotted the devastation. Chairs and tables floated in the pool, broken umbrellas had sunk to the bottom, and there was broken glass everywhere. In our desperate efforts to save Gordon's life, we had trashed the entire place!

Before we even had a chance to explain, our parents, coaches, teacher and the entire class had been thrown out of the hotel and were left standing on the street! Our luggage followed a few minutes later.

"We've called for your bus," said the furious hotel manager. "It will be here shortly. You are no longer welcome at this resort, and furthermore, I reported your wild behaviour to the organizers of the dodge ball tournament, and you've been kicked out of that, too!! He turned on his heel and stomped back into the resort.

Mrs. Hoagsbrith looked at the parents as if to say, "See what I have to put up with every day?"

No one said a word on the ride back to the airport, and our school was never again invited to a tournament away from home.

Chapter 2

The Coat of Many Colours

Our teacher, Mrs. Hoagsbrith, is a strong believer in recycling. Our classroom has a recycling box for everything from paper to juice boxes. For the past two weeks, every science lesson had been about the importance of recycling. When the lessons were finally over, Gordon raised his hand and said, "Mrs. H., you've just spent the last two weeks teaching us all about recycling. I have a question: What *can't* be recycled?"

"That's a very good question, Gordon," replied our teacher. "The answer is there's *nothing* that can't be recycled. *Everything* should be recycled."

Just then the bell rang dismissing our class for the weekend. As Gordon and I walked home, I could tell that he was in a great mood.

"What are you so happy about?" I asked him. "We have to write that book report this weekend, remember? It'll take hours and hours, and that's if you've actually read a book recently. I have to spend all day Saturday reading a book and then all day Sunday writing the report."

"Not me," grinned Gordon. "You heard Mrs. H. She said that *everything* should be recycled, so I'm going to take one of my old book reports, change a couple of words here and there and hand it back in. Think of all the ink and paper and time that will be saved. Plus, she'll be so happy that I recycled, I'll probably get a much higher mark this time."

As we continued walking, Gordon stopped some of the other kids in our class and explained his latest plan to them. Everyone thought that it was a great idea and they happily agreed to do the same thing. Before long, word spread to the rest of the class, and on Monday morning, we handed in 29 recycled book reports to our teacher.

"Wait just a minute," said Mrs. Hoagsbrith, frowning as she sorted through our papers. "I recognize these book reports. You've all turned the same reports in again. That's cheating!"

"No, it's not!" cried Gordon. "It's *recycling!*' Think of all the ink and paper our class just saved. I'll bet we saved an entire forest. Not to mention the wear and tear on the books in the library by not reading them. Now they'll last longer for everyone else to use and enjoy!" He grinned triumphantly.

When Mrs. Hoagsbrith finally finished yelling at us, she paged the principal to our classroom. When Mr. Evans arrived, she told him what we had done. His eyes bulged and his face turned red as he yelled at us some more. When he was finally through, he announced that since we were so fond of recycling, he was going to enter our class in the upcoming town-wide recycling contest. If we won, all would be forgiven, but if we lost, we would have to write a book report every week from now until the end of the school year. As it was only October, that would mean *a lot* of book reports!

"The rules of the recycling contest are simple," Mr. Evans informed us. "Your class must create a product made completely out of recycled materials. This product will then be put up for sale at the local mall alongside the products made by other people. The product that sells for the most money will win the contest. So, I suggest you get to work right away. The contest is on Saturday...*this* Saturday, so unless you want to spend your weekends from now until the end of June writing book reports, I suggest you give this contest your best effort." He turned and stormed out of the room leaving us in stunned silence.

After school, our entire class met under the big oak tree in the schoolyard to discuss our horrible situation.

"Well, Gordon," I said. "You got us into this mess. I hope you have a good plan for getting us out of it."

Twenty-eight pairs of eyes turned expectantly to Gordon. "Well?" asked Paulo. "Do you have any great ideas, or are we doomed to a whole year of writing book reports?"

"Give me a minute," replied Gordon slowly. "I've

been thinking about this all day and I have an idea. We have to make a product out of recycled material, right? Now, don't ask any questions, but I want everyone to go home and look in your dresser for your oldest, most worn-out pair of underwear. Bring them to school tomorrow. Trust me. We are going to win that contest!"

Puzzled, our class left the playground and headed for home to search for their oldest underwear. Turning to Paulo and me, Gordon said, "You guys come with me. We have to get to the mall right away to buy something."

The next morning, every kid in our class brought Gordon a pair of old, worn-out underwear. He hid them all in a green garbage bag and promised to tell us what his great plan was after school.

Right after morning announcements, Mr. Evans made a special visit to our class to ask how our recycling project was coming along. When we admitted that we hadn't actually started to make anything yet, he chuckled and said, "Well, I didn't think this class could actually come up with a product good enough to win that competition. I hope you enjoy writing book reports!" The principal left our classroom with a smile on his face, no doubt picturing us slaving away reading books and writing book reports every weekend until the end of June.

When school was finally over, our class met at Paulo's house to hear the rest of Gordon's great idea. Reaching into his backpack, Gordon pulled out a slim package. "Inside this package is a pattern for making a woman's coat," said Gordon. Our class just stared at him. What was Gordon up to?

"My plan is to have Paulo's mom take our old underwear and sew them together to make a big piece of cloth. Then she can make a coat out of it! The coat meets all of the requirements of the contest," assured Gordon. "It is a product that can be sold and it will be made entirely of recycled material. And unless one of you has a better idea, I suggest we go with this one."

Our class didn't have any better ideas, and since the contest was only a few days away, we decided to go with Gordon's idea.

"Great!" said Gordon happily, as he dumped out the bag of underwear on the floor. I looked at it with interest.

I had no idea our class wore so many different colours of underwear. There were red, purple, pink, green, yellow, orange, blue, and even stripes and polka-dots! This was going to be one weird coat, I thought.

Paulo's mother agreed to sew the coat together for us, and we decided not to tell Mr. Evans about our project. He would just have to wait and see it at the mall on Saturday.

The next morning at school, the principal visited our classroom again to remind us that there were only three days left before the contest took place. He also put a notice up on the blackboard on which he had worked out how many book reports we would have to write between now and the end of June if we didn't win the recycling competition. Our class turned and stared at Gordon with worried looks. It was a *very* big number.

By Friday, Mrs. Lima had finished the coat, and after school our whole class went over to Paulo's house to see it. The underwear coat turned out far better than we expected. For the first time, we actually thought we stood a chance at winning the recycling competition! It was the world's most colourful coat. It would be great if we could win first prize and ruin Mr. Evans' dream of making us all write book reports every week until the end of the year!

Early Saturday morning we took our coat to the mall and were given a booth in front of an expensive women's clothing store. We hung up the colourful coat for all to see. We agreed that no one would tell the big secret – that the coat was actually made out of our old underwear!

The mall soon opened and quickly filled with shoppers. More and more people stopped by our booth to admire the colourful coat. We had put a price tag of $500.00 on it, figuring that we could always lower the price if the coat didn't sell by noon. Many women tried on the coat and said they loved it, but the price was a little out of their range.

Throughout the morning, the kids in our class took turns walking around the mall to see what products other people had created. There was some artwork made out of things people had thrown out in their blue boxes, some neat model cars made entirely of bottle caps, some doll clothes that were made out of old clothes from a second-hand store, and a bunch of other things that we couldn't identify. None of the items were as expensive as ours, or as nice, for that matter. If our coat sold for $500.00, we would win the recycling competition for sure!

By noon, the mall was very busy, but our coat still hadn't sold. Just as we were going to lower the price to $450.00, Mrs. Hoagsbrith walked up to our booth. She had come to see what her class had made for the contest. Gordon proudly pointed to the colourful coat.

"This is our recycling project, and when it sells, we will win the top prize, and that means NO BOOK REPORTS FOR US!" We all cheered.

Mrs. Hoagsbrith rubbed the coat between her fingers and gasped, "It's absolutely beautiful. And so soft. What did you make it out of?"

Knowing we could trust our teacher with our secret, Gordon proudly announced, "Everybody's old undies!"

Letting go of the coat as though it were a hot potato, Mrs. Hoagsbrith said, "No one is ever going to buy a coat made of this!" She sighed, knowing just how many book reports she was going to have to mark. And then it happened. Mrs. Evans, the principal's wife, came out of the expensive women's store in front of our booth, spied our coat, and hurried over to us with her arms outstretched. Grabbing the coat with both hands, she cried, "This is wonderful. I always dreamed of owning such a colourful coat as this!" She felt the cloth with her fingers and held the coat up to her nose and breathed deeply. "Oh, it even smells wonderful. I'll buy it at any price!"

"But what will your husband say?" asked the friend she was with, checking the $500.00 price tag. "It's a very expensive coat."

"Oh, he'll just *love* it. He likes me to dress well. In fact, he's always complaining about how poorly the teachers at his school dress, especially the women. They come to work dressed in old rags practically! By the way," she continued, turning to Gordon. "What is this *amazing* coat made of?"

Before Gordon could say a word, Mrs. Hoagsbrith reached over and clamped her hand over his mouth.

"It's a secret, she said between clenched teeth. "All I

can say is that it's made out of a very rare cloth, and we're not allowed to tell you any more about it according to the rules of the recycling contest."

"Well I don't care *what* it's made out of. I simply *have* to have it," said the principal's wife, trying it on and modelling it for her friend. She pulled out her checkbook and said, "I can't wait to see the expression on my husband's face when he sees me in this fabulous coat!"

"Neither can I," grinned Mrs. Hoagsbrith. *"Neither can I!"*

Chapter 3

The Day Gordon Got Arrested

On Thursday morning as Gordon was walking to school, a large bald man hurried down a driveway and called, "Excuse me, young man. I was wondering if you could help me. My wife is at work and I seem to have locked myself out of my house. There's a window around back that's unlocked, but I'm afraid I'm too big to fit through it. Do you think you could climb through my window and then let me into my house?"

"I'd be happy to help you, sir," said Gordon, looking at his watch. "It'll just take a minute and I can still get to school in plenty of time."

"Great!" smiled the man, as he walked Gordon into the backyard, glancing around as he did so.

Laying down his backpack, Gordon stepped on a lawn chair, opened the window and climbed into the house. He dropped down into a bedroom.

"Just unlock the front door and let me in, and then you can hurry off to school," called the man from outside.

"OK," said Gordon, as he made his way through the house. He unlocked and opened the front door, expecting to see the man there, hopefully with a small reward to thank Gordon for his help. Instead, Gordon was shocked to see a muscular policeman with a pair of handcuffs in his hands!

"Caught you red-handed!" the policeman said. "I saw you breaking into this house through that window."

"N-n-no," stammered Gordon, looking around desperately for the bald man. "I was just helping out the guy who *does* live here. He locked himself out and asked me to climb through the back window and unlock the door for him!"

"Sure, sure," said the policeman in a bored tone. "I've

heard that excuse a hundred times. So just where is this man, then?"

"I don't know!" cried Gordon. "He was right here a minute ago!"

"Well, your imaginary friend seems to be nowhere in sight now," said the policeman, spinning Gordon around and placing him in handcuffs. "All I know is that I saw you breaking into this house through a window. I don't see any man, and I happen to know that a little old lady lives here all alone. So unless you can come up with a better excuse than that, I'm going to have to take you downtown and lock you up!"

Gordon's mouth went dry and he was unable to speak. As the policeman led him to the waiting cruiser, Gordon looked up and down the street frantically, hoping to catch a glimpse of the man who had gotten him into all this trouble. The street was deserted.

Gordon was locked into the back of the police car, and as it sped away, the officer turned on his siren and flashing light. Terrified, Gordon stared wide-eyed out of the window as the car rushed to the police station.

29

Rounding a corner, the car drove past our school, where the siren had drawn the attention of hundreds of kids who were lined up at the fence to see what the excitement was all about. They didn't expect to see Gordon, shaking with fear, staring blankly back at them from the back of a police cruiser!

At the station, the police wasted no time in contacting Gordon's parents at work. While he waited for them to arrive, Gordon sat in a locked cell and worried about what would happen next. Would he go to jail? Would his parents bail him out? Would anyone believe his story?

An agonizing hour went by before a door at the end of the hallway was unlocked and Gordon's parents rushed through, followed by another police officer.

"Alright, kid. Since this is your first offence, we're going to let you out in the custody of your parents. There will be a trial next week and you can tell your story to the judge then."

Gulping as he hung his head in shame, Gordon meekly followed his parents out of the police station.

*　　*　　*　　*　　*

All day long I worried about Gordon. I didn't learn a single thing and twice Mrs. Hoagsbrith had to tell me to pay attention. The minute school was over, Paulo and I ran to Gordon's house to find out what had happened.

Gordon's mother opened the door when we knocked and then invited us in.

"Gordon is in his room," she said. "I'm sure he would love some company."

"Hey, guys," said Gordon, trying to smile as we entered his room. "What's up?"

"You tell us!" I replied. "You wouldn't believe the rumours that are going around school. You're even more famous than before."

"Great," sighed Gordon sadly. He quickly told us how he had been tricked by a large bald man to break into an old lady's house. "The only good part is that my parents believe me. They know I would never break into anyone's house!"

"And you have no idea who this man was?" asked Paulo.

31

"I never saw him before in my life," moaned Gordon. "What am I going to do?"

Paulo and I stayed with Gordon for an hour, trying to cheer him up and telling him that everything would be OK. *We* knew that he was innocent. We could only hope that the judge would believe Gordon was innocent, too.

The next morning at school, Gordon was surrounded by curious kids all wanting to know what had happened. Even Mrs. Hoagsbrith believed Gordon's story, and she was extra nice to him all day. In a rare gesture of kindness, she didn't even assign our class any homework over the weekend, saying that she thought we all deserved a break, looking at Gordon as she spoke.

Gordon and I waved to Paulo as he boarded his school bus, and the two of us walked home together.

*   *   *   *   *

Fifteen minutes later, Paulo got off the bus and was walking up his driveway when he heard a voice calling to him. Turning around, he saw a large bald man in overalls at the farm across the road.

"Young man! Can you help me for a minute? I can't

seem to get this gate open. The latch is stuck, and I've come to look at some cows that I'm considering buying."

"Sure," called Paulo, jogging across the road to help the man. "That gate's always been a bit tricky. I don't know why Mr. McGregor doesn't get it fixed. Sometimes I feed his cows for him when he's away, and I always have trouble with it, too. I didn't know Mr. McGregor was selling his cows."

"Well, he just advertised them in today's newspaper. He's selling the entire herd," replied the man.

With a bit of fumbling, Paulo finally managed to unlatch the gate and swing it open.

"Thank you kindly," said the man, as he stepped into the field.

"No problem," said Paulo, and with a friendly wave, he returned home.

*   *   *   *   *

Early the next morning, Paulo was awakened by the sound of someone banging on the front door. Climbing out of bed, he glanced out of his bedroom window and saw a police car parked in the driveway. He quickly got dressed and hurried downstairs. His parents were in the kitchen, talking to a policeman. Paulo paused outside the kitchen door and listened.

"What a shame," he heard his mother say. "Mr. McGregor had the best herd of cows around here."

"Yes," agreed his father. "And they were worth a lot of money."

"Well, if you see anything suspicious, give us a call," said the policeman. "We sure want to get to the bottom of this theft. Imagine stealing cows right out of a farmer's pasture in broad daylight! And the thief didn't even bother to close the gate behind him."

Gate?! *Uh-oh,* thought Paulo. *I helped the thief steal those cows right out of Mr. McGregor's pasture!*

Deciding to say nothing to the police just yet, Paulo turned around and raced through the back door. Grabbing his bike, he quickly pedalled to my house and told me the story of the stolen cows.

"And I think the bald man that tricked me to open the gate for him is the same man that tricked Gordon into climbing through that window!" he finished excitedly.

34

"Wow!" I said. "Now all we have to do is find the guy and turn him into the police! We'll be heroes and Gordon won't have to go to jail!"

"It won't be easy," argued Paulo. "After all, how are we going to find the bald man? He's not just going to walk into the police station and confess!"

"I hadn't thought of that," I said. "We need a plan. Let's go to Gordon's house and tell him what's happened."

*   *   *   *   *

"Wow!" said Gordon when Paulo finished his story. "It's got to be the same bald man! If we can catch him, the police will *know* I'm innocent."

"Yeah, but how can *we* catch him?" I asked.

"Well, I may have a plan," said Gordon. "Listen to this..."

Gordon, Paulo and I knew that the Chief of Police owned a 1957 silver-blue Corvette in mint condition. Gordon's plan was to make up a bunch of signs advertising the Corvette for sale. We hoped the bald man would see the signs and know exactly where and when he could steal a very expensive car.

We spent the rest of the morning making signs advertising the car.

For Sale

1957 Corvette
Silver-Blue
Mint Condition

17 Maple Drive

Car can be viewed
after 6pm when I get
off work.

We then plastered them around town and crossed our fingers, hoping the bald man would see the signs and take the bait.

Next, Gordon, Paulo and I hid between the bushes at the end of the Chief's driveway, armed with a cell phone, and waited to see if the bald man would show up. A couple of hours passed, and then we spotted him! Coming down the sidewalk straight towards us was the bald man!

"That's him!" whispered Paulo excitedly.

"It sure is!" confirmed Gordon.

The man walked past our hiding spot in the bushes and up the front walk. He rang the doorbell and waited. When no one answered, he began peering around, looking through the front windows. Satisfied that no one was home, he snuck around to the garage and peeked in through the side window. With a glance over his shoulder, he pulled some tools out of his pocket and began to pick the lock on the side door of the garage.

"Call the police," whispered Paulo. "He's breaking into the garage."

I quickly dialed the police station and the Chief himself answered.

"Hello, Police Chief here."

"Hi. I'd like to report a break and enter at 17 Maple Drive," I said.

"17 Maple Drive? That's my house!!" exclaimed the Chief.

Over the phone, we could hear the Police Chief yell into his radio, "Attention, all police units! Emergency! Emergency! Go to 17 Maple Drive. I repeat, 17 Maple Drive. Someone is breaking into *my* house! *An extra week's vacation to the officer who catches the thief!*"

And then it happened. From all over town came the sound of police sirens and squealing tires as every policeman on duty sped toward 17 Maple Drive, each one wanting to be the first on the scene and get an extra week's vacation! In less than a minute, two police cars came racing bumper to bumper down Maple Drive, straight toward the bushes where Gordon, Paulo and I still remained hidden.

"Look!" yelled Paulo, pointing at the cars.

"Look over there!!" I yelled even louder, pointing at two *more* cars racing from the opposite direction. All four speeding cars were headed straight toward the Chief's driveway, and the very bushes in which we were hidden! A split second later, all four cars crashed into each other, narrowly missing us, rooted to our hiding spot.

When the dust cleared, two cruisers were upside down,

one was on fire, and the fourth was totally wrecked. Miraculously unharmed, all four officers jumped out of their vehicles, guns in one hand, night sticks in the other. They looked frantically for the thief.

"There he goes!!" I yelled, pointing as the terrified thief ran towards the back fence. All four police officers were on him in a flash. The thief was knocked to the ground. Each officer grabbed a leg or an arm, pulling the man in different directions, yelling, "Let go!! He's mine!" *"I got him first!"* "No, you didn't. *I* did!"

Gordon, Paulo and I climbed out of the bushes just as the Chief of Police pulled up in his cruiser. We saw him stare at the wrecked and burning police cars in his front yard, and then followed his gaze to the back yard, where four of his officers were playing tug-of-war with the bald man. We decided it was a good time to sneak home, but the Police Chief saw us and bellowed, "YOU BOYS! FREEZE!! Now come with me!!"

Stopping in our tracks, we turned and followed the Chief into his back yard where he ordered his men to drop the thief. The man was so terrified of being pulled apart like a wishbone by the four officers that he ran to the Police Chicf and fell to his knees. "I confess! I confess! I'm a crook! I did it! I admit tricking that boy into breaking into an old lady's house." He pointed at Gordon. "And that boy," he added, pointing at Paulo. "I tricked him into helping me steal some cows. And I tried to steal a car at this house. Take me to jail," he begged, looking at the angry officers and the wrecked police cars. "I'll never commit another crime in this town again! It's just too dangerous!!"

Chapter 4

When Grandmas Attack

It was Friday morning, and our class listened as our principal, Mr. Evans, read the morning announcements. The principal was complaining that too many kids were coming to school late every day. In the past week, he said, so many kids had been late that he was now forced to make a new school rule. Starting Monday morning, anyone who was late for school in the morning without a very good excuse would receive an automatic suspension and a week of detentions upon their return. We knew our principal really meant business because during lunch, he once again announced the new rule: Automatic suspension followed by a week of detentions if anyone was late on Monday morning. Then, at the end of the day, Mr. Evans came back on the PA system to remind us one final time, in case anyone had forgotten, that if any students were late without a very good reason, they would be automatically suspended from school and receive an additional week of detentions. No one wanted to be late on Monday morning.

Oddly enough, although he's always trying to think up ways to get *out* of school, Gordon is practically never *late* for school. Just to be on the safe side, however, we decided that we would meet five minutes earlier than usual to walk to school on Monday morning.

*　　*　　*　　*　　*

I walked to Gordon's house on Monday morning, and I was happy to see Gordon standing with his backpack outside his house ready for school. His mother was backing her car out of the driveway on her way to work when she stopped and rolled down the window.

"Gordon, I almost forgot," she called. "Grandma's

sleeping downstairs and I don't want to leave her alone in the house all day. Who knows what she might get into. Run inside and put her out in the backyard for the day, will you?"

"Sure, mom," said Gordon, setting down his backpack as his mother drove away.

"Your mom wants you to leave your poor old grandmother outside all day?" I asked in disbelief.

Gordon laughed. "No, no. It's my aunt's cat!" he explained. "The cat's name is Grandma. My aunt's on vacation and we're cat-sitting for her."

"Oh," I said, relieved that they weren't going to leave an old lady in the backyard all day. "Hurry up, though. We can't be late for school."

"Then come inside and help me put Grandma out," suggested Gordon.

We headed downstairs and found the old cat sleeping peacefully in her basket, purring softly. Gordon approached the cat with outstretched arms, and in a friendly voice said, "Good Grandma. You're going to spend the day outside."

Now Grandma may have been old and half deaf, but as soon as she heard the word 'outside' she bolted from her basket and ran to the other end of the basement with the speed of a young wildcat. She disappeared under a pile of boxes that was stored under the basement steps.

"Quick! Do something, Gordon! We've got to hurry!" I said, worried that we'd be late.

Gordon and I quickly moved boxes of old clothes and baby toys out of the way until we finally saw the cat's tail sticking out between two small crates.

"Okay," Gordon whispered. "You lift the top crate and I'll grab Grandma before she can run and hide again."

Run and hide turned out to be a game Grandma knew well. The second I touched the top crate, the cat darted out between Gordon's legs and ducked behind the furnace. Fortunately, *run and find* was a game that Gordon and I knew well. We raced to the furnace and found that Grandma had crawled into a small air vent.

"Ha! She's trapped now," said Gordon happily, dropping to his knees and shoving his hand into the vent to pull the cat out. "Ahhhhhh!" he screamed, pulling his hand quickly out of the vent. He held his arm up and I saw five deep red scratches running down his forearm.

"You just don't know how to deal with cats," I chuckled. "Let me show you how a pro does it." Instead of sticking my arm into the vent and scaring the cat, I bent down with my face close to the vent and called out in a friendly, soothing voice, "Here, Grandma, Grandma, Grandma. Here, Grandma, Grandm-ahhhhhh!!"

Without warning, the cat launched herself out of the vent and latched onto my face, her belly pressed against my mouth and nose and her claws digging into my scalp. Gordon instantly burst into laughter. I staggered around the basement, blinded by the cat's stomach, trying to shake Grandma off of my head. Finally, after much hissing and spitting, Grandma tired of the game and released her death grip on my head. She tore off and disappeared up the stairs. Gordon and I raced after her, searching each room for the cat and then closing the door behind us. Finally we came to the last room, Gordon's parents' bedroom. Sure enough, we saw the tip of Grandma's tail sticking out from under the bed, swishing angrily back and forth. As Gordon approached the bed, the cat hissed loudly. Gordon carefully lifted up the bedspread, and the cat opened her mouth into 'bite' position. Her claws were out in 'scratch' position. Clearly, she was ready for battle.

"Go and open the back door," said Gordon, backing away from the bed. "I'll get her out from under the bed and chase her toward the door. When she runs outside, you slam it shut behind her."

"Okay," I said, ready to try anything. I glanced at the alarm clock on the night table. "Holy cow! Look at the time. You'd better get that cat out quickly or we're going to be late for school!"

I ran downstairs and opened the back door, ready to slam it shut as soon as the cat ran through it. From upstairs I could hear lots of banging and hissing, and then a streak of white fur flew down the stairs and straight outside. I slammed the door shut with a satisfying bang.

Gordon and I wasted no time in grabbing our backpacks and desperately racing up the street to school. We ran into the deserted playground and straight to the

door. When I tried to yank it open, the door was locked!
We were late!!

"Two minutes after nine!" said an angry voice behind
us. We spun around to face our principal, who was
looking at his watch. "Well, boys, what's your excuse?
And it had better be good!"

"It is," gasped Gordon. "My mother said Grandma
might get up to something if we left her alone in the house
all day, but when I tried to lock her outside, she ran
behind the furnace and scratched my arm." Gordon held
his arm out for our wide-eyed principal to see.

"Then she grabbed my head and scratched me," I
added, showing the principal the scratches on my ears and
face. The principal's mouth fell open.

"Next," Gordon continued, "Grandma ran upstairs and
hid under my parents' bed, so I poked her out with a
broom and chased her outside." And then it happened.
Our principal fainted.

Chapter 5

Tooth and Bone

When little kids lose a tooth, most of them place it under their pillow and wait eagerly for the tooth fairy to come and exchange the tooth for money, but not Gordon. Gordon has saved each and every tooth he has ever lost. What he did with his old teeth was pure genius. We had learned long ago that grandmothers are the kindest and most generous of all people when it comes to kids. This, we guessed, was because they felt guilty about being strict and stingy with their own kids and were trying to make up for it while they still had time. Gordon used this guilt to his advantage. What he did was wait for an elderly woman to walk in front of the candy store. Then Gordon would come racing by on his bike and hit the curb on purpose. He would fake a nasty bike crash, sit up moaning in pain and then spit out some of his old teeth onto the sidewalk. The outcome was always the same. The old woman would rush over and smother Gordon with affection. "My dear boy, are you all right?" she would ask with concern. Then, noticing the teeth on the ground, she'd exclaim "Why, you've knocked out some teeth! And you're not even crying. You're so brave!"

It was about then that she would notice the candy store. "Maybe some ice cream would help," she'd say.

"Yes," Gordon would reply bravely. "It just might."

It was a great trick, and Gordon played it many times, but now that he was older, he could no longer get away with such a stunt. In fact, Gordon's old teeth were about to get him into some serious trouble.

We had been studying the human body in science class for several weeks and our teacher had assigned a group project. Using Popsicle sticks and toothpicks, we were to build a complete human skeleton. Gordon, Paulo and I were in the same group, and Gordon thought it would be more fun if we used real bones and teeth for our skeleton. Gordon's Uncle Ivan was a butcher and it would be easy to collect all the bones we wanted from out back at his butcher shop. Building a skeleton from real bones sounded a lot more fun than gluing Popsicle sticks together. So, after school, Gordon climbed into the dumpster behind his uncle's shop and began sorting through all the different animal bones. Paulo and I sat on the rim of the dumpster and watched as Gordon held a bone up next to his arm or leg. If it looked like a match, he would hand it up to me and I would put it in our shopping bag.

After about an hour, we had enough bones to make the best skeleton our teacher had ever seen. When we added Gordon's old teeth, we figured our collection of bones would look human enough to fool anyone.

The next morning Gordon and I walked to school. Gordon carried our shopping bag of animal bones and his old teeth. We had a few minutes to spare, so we decided to stop at the store near our school for a morning snack. As we wandered around the store, we found our favourite candy on a top shelf. Setting down the shopping bag, Gordon reached up and was just able to grab the candy with two fingers. We got in line, paid for our candy and hurried off to school, arriving just as the bell rang.

After morning announcements, Mrs. Hoagsbrith told us to take out our science project material and begin working on our group projects. We would have until recess.

"Oh, darn," said Gordon under his breath. He raised his hand. "Mrs. H., I left our science material at the store this morning."

Mrs. Hoagsbrith frowned. "Oh, Gordon!"

Suddenly her face brightened. "You know, it's only ten minutes there and back," she reasoned, delighted with the prospect of a few minutes of peace and quiet with Gordon gone. "I think it would be OK if you ran to the store and picked up your material and brought it right back to school. But try not to let anyone see you leaving the building. You really shouldn't leave the property during school time."

Ten minutes later, Gordon had not returned. Twenty minutes later Gordon had not returned. After thirty minutes and becoming very worried, Mrs. Hoagsbrith buzzed the office to report that Gordon had gone to the store on an errand and had not yet returned. We watched out the window as our principal, Mr. Evans, got in his car and sped to the store to find Gordon.

Arriving at the store, Mr. Evans was surprised to see that the entire parking lot had been taped off by the police. There were about a dozen police officers and detectives dusting for fingerprints and searching for clues. Mr. Evans spotted Gordon locked in the back of a police car. He hurried over, knocked on the glass and demanded, "Gordon, what have you done now?"

Before Gordon could answer, a young police officer approached Mr. Evans and asked, "Do you know this kid?"

"Know him? I should say so! I've helped teach him everything he knows!"

Before Mr. Evans could say another word, the police officer opened the door and threw the principal into the back of the car with Gordon. Locking the door, he yelled, "Hey, Chief! I've got another suspect!"

The Chief hurried over to check out the new suspect, and then he sighed in a weary voice, "Let him out, Officer Higgins. I know this man. He's the school principal!"

The door was unlocked. Mr. Evans stepped out of the cruiser and asked, "What's this all about, Chief?"

The Chief explained how the storeowner had found a gruesome shopping bag full of bones and teeth in his store. He immediately called the police.

"So, it looks like we've got a killer on the loose," finished the Chief.

"Wait just a minute," said Mr. Evans. "Why have you got one of my students in the back of that police car?"

"Well," said the Chief. "Just after my officers got here, he showed up, sneaking around and looking shifty and suspicious."

"Gordon always looks that way," explained Mr. Evans. "Let *me* talk to him."

The car door was unlocked, and Gordon was allowed to talk to the principal and the Police Chief.

"Gordon," asked the principal. "Did you come here looking for that shopping bag?"

"Yes," answered Gordon.

"Aha! A confession!" cried the Police Chief, taking out his handcuffs and preparing to put them on Gordon.

"Just a minute!" said the principal, raising his hands. "Gordon, why were you out of school at this time of day looking for a shopping bag full of bones and teeth?"

And then it happened.

"It was all Mrs. Hoagsbrith's fault," blurted Gordon. "She told me to come and get this bag and bring it back to school, but not to let anyone see me doing it!"

"Aha!!" yelled the Chief, pushing Gordon and the principal out of the way. "Come on, boys! I've solved the murder. The real killer is over at the school!"

The Police Chief and his officers rushed off to find Mrs. Hoagsbrith and put her in handcuffs.

Mr. Evans sighed. "I don't know what's really going on here, but when this mess you caused gets straightened out, I'll bet Mrs. Hoagsbrith is going to need an entire week off on stress leave."

"Me, too," sighed Gordon. "Me, too."

Chapter 6

Mrs. Hoagsbrith's Raise

One day, shortly after morning announcements, our principal, Mr. Evans, knocked on our classroom door and told our teacher that he wanted to have a little talk with our class in private.

Oh, no. What had we done now? we wondered.

"Oh, no. What have they done now?" Mrs. Hoagsbrith asked .

"Nothing at all," replied Mr. Evans. He paused. "At least, nothing that I know about. Why don't you give me ten minutes alone with them? Go down to the Teachers' Room and relax for a few minutes. I'll send someone to get you when we're done."

With a puzzled glance around the classroom, Mrs. Hoagsbrith left, closing the door behind her.

"Now," began Mr. Evans, looking around the room. "I have just been informed by the Superintendent that this school is going to be part of a new experiment. For quite some time, there has been a lot of talk about teachers' salaries and how much of a raise they should get."

Twenty-nine blank faces stared at our principal. Why was he telling this to us?

"The Superintendent has decided that only those teachers whose class is doing well will get a raise this year. This class, for instance, is below average. In order for your teacher to get a raise, *every one* of you will have to do much better in school. We need *each* of you to work harder. You know, completing your homework every day, getting your assignments in on time. So I've come up with a plan."

Our class let out a loud moan. No doubt Mr. Evans' plan involved a lot of extra work.

"Don't worry," he continued. "There won't be any

extra homework involved. All I am asking you to do is this. All of you will come to school a half hour early for extra lessons. Each day after school, you'll remain for an extra hour in the new study club. And finally, there will be daily tests and quizzes during recess to monitor your progress and see where you need extra help. Oh, and we'll replace your gym time with extra help in French since we *know* those marks are low.

We sat in stunned silence. Surely this was some sort of joke!

"Now," the principal continued. "I must tell you that this is strictly on a *volunteer* basis. I'm asking you to do this for your teacher. Just think how happy it would make Mrs. Hoagsbrith to have her students get higher grades and for her to get a raise in pay. So, if the entire class volunteers to follow this new program, you'll all get higher grades and Mr. Hoagsbrith will get a nice big raise. I'm leaving this up to you to decide, and I sincerely hope you do this for your teacher. Take five minutes and talk it over as a class."

Before he left the room, Mr. Evans asked Gordon to go

to the Teachers' Room after we had made our decision and ask Mrs. Hoagsbrith to return to the classroom.

A minute later, Gordon went to the Teachers' Room, knocked on the door and announced, "Mr. Evans said to tell you that you can come back now."

As the two walked down the hall together, Mrs. Hoagsbrith cleared her throat and asked, "Well, what did the principal have to say?"

And then it happened. Gordon said, "Mr. Evans just explained that there is *no way* you're getting a raise this year."

Chapter 7

When Teachers Attack!

"Life is so unfair to kids," complained Gordon as we walked home from school one day, our backpacks heavy with homework.

"In what way?" I asked him.

"Well, did you ever notice how we always celebrate Mother's Day and Father's Day? There's even Grandparent's Day! What makes *them* so special? How come there's no Kid's Day?"

"My mother says that *every* day is Kid's Day," said Paulo.

"Hah!" exclaimed Gordon. "Well, I'm not going to

60

wait around for someone to invent Kid's Day. I'll probably be an adult by then. I'm going to start it myself! Tomorrow will be the first Official Kid's Day, and to celebrate it, I'm *not* going to go to school!"

"Gordon," I warned, "if you don't show up at school tomorrow, they'll call your parents, and then you'll be in BIG trouble."

Gordon smiled and said, "Oh, yeah? Wanna bet? I've been thinking about it all day and I already have that part all figured out. Remember last week when I was sick? My dad phoned the school and all he said was, 'Hello. This is Mr. Smith. Gordon is sick today and won't be able to come to school.' Then he hung up. *It's as easy as that.* Tomorrow morning, all I have to do is phone the school and pretend to be my dad! Then I can spend the whole day celebrating Kid's Day!"

"What are you going to do all by yourself?" asked Paulo cautiously, sensing what was coming next.

"I won't be all by myself!" said Gordon with a grin. "You guys will be right there with me celebrating the first ever Official Kid's Day!"

"I knew it," groaned Paulo. "Gordon, if you think I'm going to play hooky with you, you can just forget it!"

"Yeah," I agreed. "Every time we let you talk us into one of your ideas, we end up in major trouble."

"Don't be a chicken!" teased Gordon. "Years from now when people ask you what you did on the first Official Kid's Day, you don't want to have to tell them that you were a big chicken and went to school, do you? Come on. It's foolproof! What could possibly go wrong?"

"Well," I said, weakening. "I don't know. What do you think, Paulo?"

"Well," said Paulo with a heavy sigh. "I don't want to miss out on the first Official Kid's Day. I guess I'll do it if you'll do it."

"Alright, Gordon, you talked me into it. I'll do it, too," I sighed as we crossed Rubicon Street and headed toward Gordon's house.

*   *   *   *   *

The next morning, I waited until both my parents were busy before I picked up the phone and called the school. I was so scared that my heart was pounding and my palms were sweaty. Maybe I really *was* getting sick. The phone rang several times, and then something wonderful happened. The school's answering machine came on and said, "Hello. This is Principal Evans. You have reached Danglemore Public School. There's no one available to take your call at the moment. Please leave a message after the beep." A few seconds went by and then there was a loud *beeep*.

In my deepest voice, I left a message on the school's answering machine saying that I was my dad and that my son had the flu and wouldn't be coming in today. Then I quickly hung up and jumped for joy. It had worked! Gordon was a genius. No school today! It was Kid's Day!!

I left the house at my usual time with my backpack slung over my shoulder. Instead of heading for school, however, I walked to the shopping mall near my house and joined Paulo and Gordon who were already waiting for me in the food court with three cold drinks.

We raised our cans of pop, clinked them together and

said, "To Kid's Day!"

"Well," I said, looking at my watch. "I wonder what all those losers at school are doing right now?"

Gordon chuckled. "They're probably doing math problems, like, how many chickens does it take to go to school every day? Ha! Ha!"

We had outsmarted our parents, the principal, and our teacher. Grinning at each other, we took big gulps from our drinks. All of a sudden, Gordon began choking on his drink and pop shot right out of his nose! He turned red and gasped for breath.

In an emergency situation like this, Paulo and I knew exactly what to do. We both pointed at Gordon and laughed at him hysterically.

"Look!" he gasped when he finally got his breath back and could talk again. "Behind you over there!"

Paulo and I turned around. It was our turn to gasp for air! Walking through the food court with a tray in her hands was none other than our teacher, Mrs. Hoagsbrith, and she was coming straight towards us!

We immediately put our faces down, hoping she

wouldn't see us. Luckily, she walked right past us and took a seat at a nearby table with another woman.

"Quick!" urged Paulo. "Let's get out of here!"

We snuck out of the food court and made it safely to the parking lot.

"That was too close," I said, wiping sweat from my brow. "Can you imagine the trouble we'd be in if she had seen us?"

"Yeah," agreed Gordon. "We'd have been in bi—" Gordon stopped mid-sentence. "Hey! Wait a minute! Why isn't *she* at school today??"

"I'll bet she's just *pretending* to be sick just so she can go shopping with her friend!" said Paulo.

"She's a cheater!" cried Gordon, squeezing his hand into a fist and shaking it. "If there's one thing I hate, it's a cheater."

"Uh, Gordon, what do you think *we're* doing?" I reminded him.

Gordon looked at me completely shocked. "It's not the same thing at all!" he argued. "We're just kids and we're still *learning* what's right and wrong. But she's a teacher so she already *knows* this is wrong. So I say that we let *her* get in trouble for a change. Let's send *her* to the principal's office and see how *she* likes it."

"What exactly do you plan on doing?" I asked warily, knowing that somehow it would involve Paulo and me.

"I'm not sure, but just follow me and we'll see what she's up to," he said, as he re-entered the mall and went directly to the food court.

Hiding behind a large artificial tree, we spied on our teacher and her friend while they finished their breakfast. At a nearby table, a baby started crying at the top of its lungs.

"Oh, don't you just hate the sound of a crying baby?" asked her friend.

"Absolutely," agreed Mrs. Hoagsbrith. "Almost as much as I hate the sound of noisy kids! If there's one thing I can't stand, it's children. To tell you the truth, I've secretly hated children my whole life!"

"Yes," said her friend, warming to the theme. "They're such noisy, messy creatures!"

"My life would be a lot nicer without kids in it," sighed

Mrs. Hoagsbrith.

Gordon, Paulo and I couldn't believe our ears. Had we really just heard our teacher say that she hates kids?

At that exact moment, our teacher suddenly spied us crouched behind the tree with our jaws open in shock.

"Speaking of kids, look at those three over there," she said, pointing at us.

"Well, don't just stand there with your mouths open," called her friend. "What have you got to say for yourselves, spying on us?"

Gordon, Paulo and I were speechless. We didn't know what to do or say. Then Gordon snapped out of it and jumped into action. He ran over to their table and snatched our teacher's credit card and the bill for her food right off the tray and shouted,

"Aha!! This bill has your signature on it, so it *proves* that you were in the food court this morning and not at home sick! When I show this to the principal, you'll wish you'd never met me!"

"I *already* wish I'd never met you," said our teacher angrily, standing up and flexing muscles much bigger than

I remembered her having.

Gordon, Paulo and I turned and ran out of the food court.

"Stop! Thief!!" shouted Mrs. Hoagsbrith. "That boy just stole my credit card!"

Several people tried to grab us as we raced out of the mall, but we shook them off and raced into the parking lot. I turned, and to my horror, saw that our teacher was quickly gaining on us with a murderous look on her face. I couldn't believe how fast she was!

"Come on!!" shouted Gordon. "Head for the school! We have to show this to the principal!"

Three minutes later, Gordon, Paulo and I sprinted into the schoolyard. Mrs. Hoagsbrith was getting closer and closer, and we were almost within her reach.

"Give me back my credit card!" she roared as Gordon yanked open the school door and we dashed towards the principal's office.

"Hurry! We've got to get this evidence to the principal, and he'll protect us!" yelled Gordon.

We burst into the office and the three of us shouted at

the startled secretary.

"Quick! Where's Mr. Evans?"

"He's out of the building at a meeting," she said.

"AHHHHHHH!" we all shouted.

"To our classroom!" yelled Gordon. "The Supply Teacher will protect us!!"

We ran down the hall towards our classroom. Suddenly Mrs. Hoagsbrith leapt from around a corner and grabbed at us. Gordon, Paulo and I crashed into some lockers and narrowly managed to keep out of her clutches.

"I'll get you!" she shouted.

We raced up the stairs and burst in on our startled class with Mrs. Hoagsbrith right on our heels. The supply teacher was at the board, her back to the room.

"Quick!! Help us!!" yelled Gordon to the supply teacher. "Mrs. H. is after us!" And then it happened.

Just as Mrs. Hoagsbrith burst into the room behind us, the *real* Mrs. Hoagsbrith turned around and spotted the woman in the doorway. "Oh," she said calmly. "I see you boys have met my twin sister. And weren't you three supposed to be sick in bed today??"

Chapter 8

The Badge

It was the best of times - a beautiful sunny Friday afternoon and the school bell had just rung, dismissing us for the weekend. Unfortunately, it was also the worst of times - Report Card day.

Everyone in our class had been given a sealed envelope with our report cards in them. Our parents were supposed to read our report cards and sign the last page as proof that we had actually brought them home. Then, on Monday, we were to return the signed page to our teacher.

Gordon and I thought we would delay giving our parents our report cards for a while by going to Paulo's house to help him with his farm chores. In addition to running their small farm, both of Paulo's parents had full time jobs, so Paulo always had to feed the animals and clean the stalls when he got home from school.

Just as we were finishing the farm chores, I looked out of the barn door and saw a large black car pull into the driveway.

"Hey, Paulo," I said, pointing to the car, "you have company."

Putting our brooms down, Gordon, Paulo and I left the barn and went out to greet the visitor. We noticed a sign on the side of his car. It said: *Special Farm Agent.*

A tall, important-looking man got out of the car and shut the door. He shook his head in disapproval as he looked around at the farm buildings, carefully removing his leather driving gloves.

"Hi," said Paulo, extending his hand toward the man. "I'm Paulo Lima and I live here. Can I help you?"

Ignoring Paulo's hand, the man sighed and removed his sunglasses. "Who owns this farm?" he asked curtly.

"My mom and dad do," said Paulo. "They're at work

right now, but they'll be home soon."

"I'm a Special Farm Agent sent by the government. I'm here to inspect every inch of this entire farm to make sure that no farm regulations are being violated."

"Well, OK, I guess," replied Paulo. "But can you wait until my parents get home? I don't think they'd want you just wandering around our farm."

Pulling a shiny badge out of his pocket and holding it six inches from Paulo's face, the Agent barked, "This badge gives me the power to inspect any farm anywhere, anytime that I want, and I wait for no one!"

"Hey," I said, trying to be helpful. "His parents will be here in 20 minutes. Can't you even wait 20 minutes?"

Instantly the Agent snapped the badge three inches in front of my face. "See this badge? It gives me the power to search this entire farm, all the fields and even the house any time I want."

"Well, then," said Gordon, "I guess you don't have to wait for Paulo's parents to come home after all. But if I were you, I'd stay out of that field over there." Gordon pointed to the field at the far end of the farm.

The badge was instantly pressed into Gordon's nose. "This badge gives me the power to go anywhere I want. And I won't have any dumb kid telling me what field to stay out of. Now get out of my way," he snarled, elbowing us aside. "I'm going to start my inspection in that very field, and if anything illegal is going on, I'll soon put a stop to it!"

The man opened the gate and marched directly to the field that Gordon had warned him to stay out of. Grinning at each other, Gordon, Paulo and I climbed on the fence and sat down to watch as the Special Farm Agent crossed the field and disappeared over a hill. And then it happened. We heard a loud yell and a moment later we saw the Special Farm Agent racing back over the hill at top speed. Close behind him, and closing fast, came Brutus, the Lima's huge bull, snorting and looking very, *very* angry.

"Serves him right," Gordon said. "I tried to warn him."

As the bull head-butted the Inspector from behind, sending him sailing through the air and over the fence,

Gordon cupped his hands around his mouth and yelled, "Show him your badge! Show him your badge!"

Chapter 9

Grounded For A Month

I hate to admit it, but if you look up *genius* in the dictionary, there should be a picture of Gordon.

A great party had been planned for Saturday night and all the kids in our class were invited. It was going to be a pool party followed by a sleepover. Everyone had been invited, all the boys *and* the girls, too. At first our parents thought the party sounded like fun, but once they heard that the girls had also been invited, they weren't so sure.

"A mixed party at your age?" said my mom skeptically.

"But everyone's going!" I argued.

"We'll see…" she said.

Every kid knows what 'we'll see' means. It means that your parents are going to see what excuse they can come up with for not letting you do something that you really want to do. In this case, 'we'll see' meant that my mom phoned Gordon's mom, who in turn phoned Paulo's mom, and it was agreed by all three of them that a mixed party at our age was not appropriate, and that the three of us wouldn't be going.

We tried arguing and begging, but their minds were made up.

"Okay," said Gordon. "If we can't go to the party, can we at least go camping overnight in the woods?" Our parents had let us do this several times in the past, and we figured that they might agree to it again. To our delight, they did. Little did they suspect that we had other plans…

* * * * *

Gordon, Paulo and I spent the next couple of days getting our gear together and packing our tent, sleeping bags, and food into a couple of big backpacks. Gordon's dad was going to drive us to the woods and then we would hike the last couple of kilometres to our camping spot. The fishing was pretty good there, so we would be bringing our rods and tackle boxes as well.

*   *   *   *   *

Friday finally arrived, but as luck would have it, Mrs. Hoagsbrith, assigned our class a ton of homework. We tried to protest, telling her that there was a great party planned for the weekend, but she said that we were behind in our schoolwork. With report cards just around the corner, we had to spend some extra time on the weekend doing homework. No amount of groaning, pleading or begging would change her mind.

That afternoon, our class left school weighed down with textbooks and assignments.

We said goodbye to Paulo as he boarded his bus.

"Remember, my dad will pick you up at 5:00 tonight. Make sure you have all your stuff ready!" called Gordon.

"Sure thing," replied Paulo as the bus pulled out of the schoolyard.

Gordon and I walked home, talking not about our upcoming camping trip, but the upcoming party that we would be attending instead. You see, our plan was to have Gordon's dad drop us off near the woods and then we'd hike in a few hundred metres and hide our fishing tackle and rods behind some bushes. Then we would hike back out with our sleeping bags and tent and head to the party. The next afternoon, when Gordon's dad arrived to pick us up, we'd be waiting by the side of the road near the woods with our gear. It was a simple plan, and it was foolproof. Once again, I had to hand it to Gordon.

When we reached Gordon's house, we were grumbling about the amount of homework our teacher had given us. Gordon's mother was home, and she overheard us talking.

"When will you get all this homework done if you're camping and fishing for half the weekend? Maybe you should cancel your trip," she said.

"No!" Gordon practically shouted. "I mean, we could take it with us and do some before we go to bed tonight."

His mother eyed us suspiciously. "Before you go to bed tonight, huh?" she asked. "Alright, I guess there's no need to cancel your trip then."

Relieved, Gordon and I rushed off to get the last of our

gear ready. Once we were safely in Gordon's room with the door closed, we took our school backpacks and stuffed them in his closet, homework already completely forgotten. Imagine ruining a perfectly good party with homework!

At ten minutes to five, our camping gear, rods and tackle boxes were sitting by the back door and Gordon and I were waiting on the driveway for Mr. Smith to get home from work to take the three of us to the woods. As soon as we saw the van coming down the street, we ran inside and grabbed our gear.

We picked up Paulo shortly after five o'clock and headed straight to the woods.

"Have a good time, boys," he called out to us once we had unloaded our gear and were ready to head into the woods.

"Thanks for the ride!" we called. "See you tomorrow at three!"

Gordon's dad left the parking lot and we grabbed our tackle boxes, rods and packs and headed down the path into the woods.

After about 5 minutes, we figured we had gone far enough to safely hide our gear.

"That looks like a good spot right over there," I said, pointing to a thick patch of bushes.

"Great," agreed Gordon. "These tackle boxes sure are heavy!"

We stowed our stuff behind the bushes, and when we were satisfied that no one would find them and steal them, we headed back out of the woods with our sleeping bags and tent and headed for the party!

*   *   *   *   *

The party was great. There was lots of food, loud music, and swimming. No one went to bed before four a.m. The next morning we all slept in late, and when we got up, there was more swimming and eating. Around noon, the party broke up, and Gordon, Paulo and I headed back to the woods to pick up our tackle boxes and rods and wait for our ride home.

An hour later, we heard the sound of a van pulling into the parking lot near the woods, and sure enough, there was Gordon's mom.

"Hi, boys!" she called out as the van pulled up beside us. "How was your night?"

"Great!" we all chorused. "We had a really fun time."

"How was the fishing?" she asked.

"That was great, too," I said.

"Yeah, I can't remember when we've had more fun," said Gordon, and then it happened.

"That's good," said Mrs. Smith. "I thought all that homework might spoil your fun."

"Homework?" asked Paulo. "I didn't bring any with me."

"Uh, yeah," stammered Gordon. "And we forgot ours in my bedroom, so I guess we'll have to do it all tomorrow."

"That's funny," said Gordon's mom with a puzzled look on her face. "I thought for sure you'd be doing some homework on this trip. When I saw that you had *forgotten* your homework in your closet, I put it in your tackle boxes. You must have noticed it when you opened them up to go fishing."

Gordon and I looked at each other, not knowing what

to say. We were caught red-handed in a lie! Gordon's mom had outsmarted us!!

Chapter 10

Big Luke

It was the middle of July, and Gordon, Paulo and I had spent the first two weeks of summer vacation pursuing one of our favourite hobbies - fishing. We fished every good spot we knew but we were having very little luck. Most days we didn't catch anything, and we were getting discouraged. We tried new lures. We tried different times of the day, and Paulo even bought a brand new rod with the money he earned selling eggs at the end of his driveway every morning, but even with that, we couldn't catch anything.

"Maybe it's too hot for the fish to bite," I grumbled as we rode our bikes home from another day of catching nothing.

"Maybe the rivers and ponds around here are just fished out," said Paulo, disappointed that his new rod had failed to catch a thing all day.

"I think we need to try some new spots," suggested Gordon. "Someplace far away from town where no one goes. A river that hasn't been fished a lot lately."

"I don't know about you guys," gasped Paulo as we pedalled up a particularly steep hill, "but I'm getting tired of these long bike rides. If we go any further, we won't have time to fish."

As it was, we were spending more and more time *getting* to the fishing spots than actually fishing. By the time we rode our bikes there and fished for an hour or so, it was time to turn around and head back home for dinner.

It was Gordon who solved the problem. When we arrived at his house, we found Gordon's mom and dad sitting in the shade of their backyard sipping cool drinks.

"Hey, dad," asked Gordon. "Could you drive us to the

river tomorrow with our bikes in the van so that we can spend more time fishing and only have to bike back home? All of the good spots near town are fished out and we need to go further away to try our luck."

"Let me get this straight," said his father, placing his empty glass on the table. "You want me to drop you kids off far away from town so you can spend the whole day fishing?" He looked at Gordon's mom, and a smile came to both their faces. "That's sounds great, boys! When do we leave?"

My gosh, I thought. *It's nice to see someone's parents being so good and kind to their son. I wished my parents were here to see such great parenting in action.*

Early the next morning, just as it was getting light out, Gordon's dad dropped the three of us off at a bridge on a deserted road far from town. I could hear the gurgling of rapids and rushing water as soon as I stepped out of the van. This sure seemed like an excellent spot to catch fish. As Gordon's dad sped away, we hid our bikes and backpacks under the bridge and headed eagerly for the river.

The next four hours were the best fishing Gordon, Paulo and I ever had. We caught lots of huge fish. It had been a great morning. The sun shone brightly and it was the hottest day of the summer. The only bad part was, it was now noon and we still had a very long, hot bike ride home. We walked back to our bikes to begin our long ride.

"Did either of you guys remember to bring any water?" asked Paulo, rooting around in his backpack.

Gordon searched his backpack and came up empty as well. "I can't believe I forgot to bring any water!" exclaimed Gordon. Looking in my pack, I found the bottle of water that I *had* remembered to pack, still a bit cool from being in the freezer over night.

Now, I have spent years in school where I was always being taught how good it is to share. If there's one thing I have learned, it's that when you share, you get less, sometimes a lot less. As I listened to Gordon and Paulo complain about how thirsty they were, I knew there was only one thing to do. In one quick movement, I slipped the water bottle from my pack and hid it out of sight under my t-shirt.

"Hey, guys, I gotta go relieve myself behind those bushes over there," I said as I hurried off to drink my cold water alone.

As I stepped behind some bushes and was unscrewing the lid on my water bottle, I heard quick footsteps behind me and knew that I had been caught red-handed. I quickly tried to gulp down all the water but I was too slow. Gordon let out a yell and grabbed me from behind in a bear hug. Paulo grabbed at me from the front, trying to grab my water bottle. The three of us fell to the ground and I dropped the water bottle. All of the cool water splashed out, soaking the ground.

"Now look what you've done!" I yelled, picking up the empty bottle. "And to think, I was just going to take a few sips myself and then share the rest with my two best friends!"

"Yeah, right!" grumbled Paulo.

"Now we have a 30 kilometre bike ride ahead of us and no water," said Gordon. "My mouth's so dry, I can hardly swallow."

87

Sighing, we gathered up our rods and backpacks and began the long ride home.

The sun beat down on us as we biked along the dusty gravel road. So far, not even one car had passed us and we hadn't seen any houses where we could stop and ask for water.

An hour passed, and I was just about to say that I couldn't go on any further when Gordon came to an abrupt stop. "Look!" he shouted, pointing ahead. "I think it's a restaurant!"

I strained to see what he was pointing at, and sure enough, I could just make out a small wooden building in the distance.

"Do either of you have any money?" asked Paulo.

"Well, no," said Gordon, "but I'm sure they'd give us some water for free if we asked. Let's go!"

Paulo and I followed Gordon down the road and into the gravel parking lot of the restaurant. It was filled with about a hundred monster trucks and motorcycles. The building itself looked very old. The paint was peeling and several shingles were missing from the roof.

Leaning our bikes against a wall, we made our way to the front door of the restaurant. A faded wooden sign read "NO KIDS ALLOWED." Clearly we were not welcome.

"Well," said Gordon. "How do you like that? Let's sneak around back and see if we can find a hose we can drink from."

To our delight, we saw a garden hose. To our horror, we also saw a large pit bull dog sleeping behind it, chained to a doghouse.

"Oh, no," I said. "What do we do now?"

"I guess we have no choice," sighed Gordon. "We have to go into the restaurant and ask for some water. I don't think I can pedal another kilometer without a drink."

Paulo and I weren't sure we liked that plan.

"After all," I reminded Gordon, "the sign said NO KIDS ALLOWED."

We argued back and forth for a while, Gordon for going inside and asking for water, and Paulo and me for staying outside and dying of thirst.

Finally Gordon said, "Well, you can stay out here if you like, but I'm going in." He started back toward the front of the restaurant. Paulo and I glanced at each other and knew that we couldn't let Gordon go in there alone. Sighing heavily, we followed him.

We slowly pushed open the door and peered cautiously inside. It took a minute for our eyes to adjust from the bright sunshine outside to the dark, smoky room. There was loud angry-sounding music playing from a radio on the counter and dozens of large, tattooed men sat around tables, talking and drinking from huge glasses.

"Looks OK to me," whispered Gordon as the three of us stepped into the restaurant. The door swung shut behind us, blocking out the light from outside and making the room even darker.

All of a sudden, the man behind the counter noticed us standing there and he turned off the music. The room instantly fell silent as all conversation stopped and every big, hairy man turned to stare at us. Timidly, Gordon stepped forward and said, "Sorry to trouble you, but could my friends and I please have some water?"

Before anyone could answer, a panic-stricken man burst through the door behind us. He had a terrified look on his

face and he shouted, *"RUN FOR YOUR LIVES,*
EVERYONE!! BIG LUKE IS COMING!!"

At once every man in the room leapt up and ran for his
life toward the door. Gordon, Paulo and I were knocked
over like bowling pins in their rush to get out of the
restaurant and save themselves from Big Luke. Truck
doors slammed, engines raced and trucks and motorcycles
peeled out of the parking lot, raising a cloud of dust.
Picking ourselves up after the stampede, we looked
around the deserted restaurant at all the knocked over
chairs and tables.

"Hurry!!" said Gordon. "Let's grab some water and
get out of here before this Big Luke guy shows up!"

And then it happened. Just as we were heading around
the counter to the sink, the door burst open once again and
the biggest, meanest, scariest-looking man we had ever
seen ran into the room. He was nearly seven feet tall and
weighed about 350 pounds. He strode over to the bar in
three huge steps and grabbed the nearest bottle. Biting off
the cap with his teeth, he chugged the drink down in
seconds. Terrified, Gordon, Paulo and I stood rooted to

the spot, praying he wouldn't notice us, but he did!

"BOY!" he shouted, pointing at Gordon. "DON'T JUST STAND THERE!! GET ME ANOTHER DRINK *NOW*!!!"

Shaking with fear, Gordon grabbed the nearest bottle and with trembling hands, he held it out to the giant man, who tore it roughly out of his hands, bit off the cap and drained the contents. Wiping his mouth with the back of his huge hairy hand, he smashed the bottle on the floor and looked around the deserted room.

With a trembling voice, Gordon stammered, "W-w-would you like another drink, sir?"

"NO TIME!" yelled the man. "WE ALL GOTTA GET OUTTA HERE!! HAVEN'T YOU BOYS HEARD? ***BIG LUKE'S HEADING THIS WAY!!!***"